The Mental Body

By Patsy Stanley

This book is about the mental body; the four divisions of energy and their time frames within our mental body.

"Time and space form the sensibilities that bound our experiences. Our senses are enclosed in the field of time and space, and our minds are enclosed in frames of categories of thought. But the ultimate thing (which is nothing) that we are trying to get in touch with is not so enclosed. We enclose it as we try to think of it."

-Joseph Campbell-

"We are all participating in the same ticks of the clock..."

-Neil Degrasse Tyson-

Before a human being manifests on planet Earth, they must make a covenant with the planet. They must agree that their soul will participate in more than just their own personal growth. Each soul makes a covenant to participate as needed in forwarding the evolution involving planet Earth as well as their personal evolution. This agreement has to take place with every form of life that manifests here.

On the soul planes, where we are older than we are anywhere else, each human being must agree to experience and express a portion of what goes on for the rest of the humanity they are a part of, (participate in mass consciousness) as well as keeping their planetary and personal agreements. This threefold agreement sets up the universal, planetary, and personal time frames that human will live in, and is one of the most basic ways human beings are alike.

These covenants govern every part of Life, and every part of life contains this agreement. So it is that we interact and learn from each other and from all of the other life forms in this classroom of life, where we visit, but never stay.

We all deal with time. We are connected to the universe we live in. We are a part of it. The materials we are made of are from different universal time frames. The energy we receive from the Sun right now is ten million years old. The universe is estimated to be 13.8 billion years old. Next, there are the ages of the Galaxy and the Cosmos in our solar system to be considered. Planet Earth is estimated to be four and a half billion years old. We are made of atoms from all those different time frames. The Sun, galaxy, cosmos, universe– these are what we are made of. How beautiful is that?

We are a combination of time frames, little bits from of universe, walking around, experiencing and expressing being Hue-man. In Hue-mans, our physical connections to time reside in the brain. Awareness of and functioning of time frames can be accessed through our conscious awareness.

Our conscious awareness resides and operates through the four bodies we have on the energy planes. All of our bodies residing on the energy planes are connected to each other, the Earth, the universe, and to the Life we are going to live here. Each of those bodies (or parts of the hue-man self), has charge of the experiencing and expression of specific time frames.

Here are our four basic energy bodies:

1. **The Soul Body**
   This body represents the ways we all have in common. The ways that we are all like each other. The fire element governs the soul body. From a spiritual perspective, fire represents our passions, compulsion, zeal, creativity, and motivation. Fire has great power for forging will and determination. It is our inner light as well as a living symbol of the Divine fire that burns in every soul.

2. **The Mental Body**
   The mental body represents the larger mind of humanity on Earth and mass consciousness. The mental body is governed by the air element. From a spiritual perspective, the air element represents the mind, knowledge, thinking, mentality, masculine energy, lightness, ether, action, movement, imagination and ideas.

The mental body resides just below the lower soul planes. This area is the storage center for the essences of all the lives we have lived so far. These storage centers are divided into time frames, and can be accessed through the brain, the physical connection to, and the representation of our mind and the mental body.

3. **The Astral Body.**

The astral or emotional body represents the larger heart of humanity. This is the home of the Child who keeps the hearth of time swept clean and in balance. This inner force is most powerful and will do what is necessary to keep each hue-man in balance so that they do not implode or explode. The astral body is governed by the water element. Water is associated with all emotions, changing time, healing, philosophy and art.

4. **The Physical Body**.

The physical body represents the outpouring of the individuality each hue-man is experiencing. The physical body has its own needs and awareness's just as all other bodies do. It is governed by the Earth Element. The Earth Element is often associated with conscientiousness, perseverance, caution, carefulness, and the care of the physical body, which has to deal with the manifestation of the energies falling through time.

The physical body manifests awareness through the five senses and its connections to the other energy bodies. Each part of the physical body is connected to its energy bodies. The mental body is connected to and manifests through the brain system.

Emotions ride the endocrine system and reside in the solar plexus. The soul body governs higher thinking and sacred rituals.

Each of our four vehicles for experiencing and expressing life resides on an energy plane with subdivisions. Different belief systems assign different numbers to the sub divisions on each of our energy planes.

In this book, our focus is on the Mental Body.

The mental body is the vehicle of experience and expression for the life energies that correspond to the mental planes of energy in human beings.

Our mental bodies are governed by the Air Element.
Our mental bodies are filled with clear, fast, cool energies. These energies assist us to think clearly.

Our brain is not our mental body. The brain is a storage center in our physical body that is connected to, and utilized by our mental body. The mind is what many people call their mental body but it is not.

The brain is the major connection point in the physical body that the activities of the mental body pour through. Do not limit learning by thinking the brain is all there is to our mental body, for it is not. The mental body is much more. It is very possible for a person with physical brain damage or suffering from a mental illness to have a perfectly healthy, unimpaired mental body.

Our mental body is never neutral. It never has been. It cannot take that position. It isn't able to. The mental body is a powerful tool that either works for or against us. There is no in between.

The Four Time Divisions of the Mental Body

Our mental body stores the essence of all the information we have collected during all of our lifetimes so far. It stores that information in four different storage units- time centers.

1. **The Future Time Storage Center** stores the files for working with the energies of the super-conscious part of the mind.

2. **The Now Time Storage Center** stores the files for Working with the energies of the conscious- part of the mind.

3. **The Lifetime Storage Center** –stores and works with the energies of the sub-conscious part of the mind.

4. **The Past Life Storage Center** is the largest storage center in the mental body. It works with the unconscious. It stores and works with the energies of every lifetime we have lived so far.

How Each Time Frame Functions:
We begin with the fastest level of energy vibration of the mental body, the super conscious mind center.

1. Future Time–The Super-conscious Mind

As the nose of a rocket leads the way, so does this part of the mental body lead the way into our future through its workings. Above the mental body reside the lower soul planes and their faster moving energies. Because of this relationship, it requires our lower soul to help plan our future.

The super conscious mind's job is to bring the future into manifestation by using the energies sent to it from the conscious mind, the now time energies that reside below it, and the soul energies residing above it, the spiritual energies. In return, the super conscious part of the mental body vibration that resides just below the lower soul plane energies, organizes those energies and sends them arcing up into the lower soul planes where they are picked up by the higher soul planes and examined. At the same time, the energies arc down into the third chakra to be properly distanced and placed. The super conscious mind is home base for the third chakra objective observer, who reports and gathers the new information, organizes and files it.

The super conscious part of the mental body is the fastest, highest in vibration and the least weighty of the mental time sections.

This part secures your future as best it can. When you are in danger, this is the mental body part that calculates everything it needs to do at lightning speed to keep you safe. This is also the home of projection, conceptual awareness, and spiritual awareness of any kind.

The super conscious mind lures us forward into the future, out of our old programming, using the faith and hope distilled and dropped down in measures through the spiritual expansion taking place constantly through the right frontal lobe of the brain.

This distillation drops down through the higher soul planes into the lower soul planes and feeds into the mental body. That is why therapists need to learn to work with who you are, and learn your spiritual nature, if they are to successfully help you change your life.

A few symbols of people and other things representing the super conscious aspect of the mental body are:

- ¬ The prophet
- ¬ The soothsayer
- ¬ Science fiction information, Star Wars, Star Trek
- ¬ Spock
- ¬ NASA as a group
- ¬ Sci-fi books
- ¬ inventions
- ¬ Anything futuristic.

The activities of filling in appointment books, planning a vacation, and dreaming about what we will be when we grow up, are just a few of the activities this part of the mental body engages in.

2. Now Time- The Conscious Mind

Now we move on to the second part of the mental body. Its rate of vibration is slower than the super conscious mind above it, but faster in vibration than the sub conscious mind below it.

The conscious mind is the tool we use to process the energy of what is going on right now. The time frame is the present, the *Now*, and it is the home of our specific focus of attention. This is the part of the mental body that sends alerts to the super conscious when you are in danger. The super conscious speeds up, and its rate of vibration increases in order to save you. Much of the programming for what is dangerous to you and should be avoided is instinctive. The rest is patterned into the sub-conscious part of you by your parents, current lifetime environments, and the situations and people you encounter.

The conscious mind automatically acts and reacts from the strong programs and patterns of the sub conscious mind, which contains all the programming we have received this lifetime so far.

Our sub conscious programming runs the show until we become aware of it, and go out on quest to find ways to change it to something more viable for us. Our subconscious programming contains many experiences that need to be thrown out, reframed, refined, or updated. Until we free up our consciousness to work on the subconscious programming stored in our mental storage center that doesn't work for us anymore, our conscious mind stays limited in what it can tell us to feel or do about life.

The subconscious mind controls more than half of our conscious awareness, and constantly directs that awareness into the old patterns it contains, until we change it. Those patterns cause us to react like our parents did to life. But the time they lived is very different than the times we live in, so what worked for them, can't work for us. What does work for us is a good overhaul and updating of our subconscious programming.

It's sort of like trying to follow the outdated religions that formed their ideas about how humanity should live in a time frame when people still believed the Earth was flat, the sun revolved around us, and there were no roads or effective means of communication to other parts of the world. Those religions and their belief systems became exclusive to one group of people, and one limited life style, utilizing a rigid set of archaic rules. That's sort of the same type of programming that parents automatically program their children with.

Subconscious programming that hasn't been worked on keeps us asleep, keeps us in a trance state. We can't study life when we are asleep and living on psychological automatic.

When we change our programming, we get positive results. We become more in touch with what is really going on with us. We learn that it is okay to take the opportunities that come our way; to experience and express Life from our own Being, not from someone else's perspective.

Our world is not the same world our parents patterned us to live in. There are many more choices available in today's rapidly changing world than they could have ever imagined.
Creating more choices than you were programmed with will create more choices in your world than you ever dreamed of. That's what matters.

Learn how your mind works, and its makeup. Learn your motivations, realize where you are going, and where it is you want to go. Discover the reasons you are limited in the amount and types of choices you have, and change them. This work is directly connected to every variety of positive growth you can imagine. As you change your subconscious programming, your conscious mind frees up and begins to work with the super conscious mind to create a new future for you.

On the spiritual planes of energy, developing conscious awareness is a part of your personal evolution. It is a learning, connective, ongoing process. Do not fight the pacing of your individual life process in this classroom of life, for you chose it. The energy centers in your bodies will open slowly and steadily, staying in unison with the lessons you are learning about life. These lessons are learned a piece at a time, to keep the chakras opening slowly and steadily and safely, so that you are not damaged by too much energy pouring into your system at one time.

The Sanskrit word *Chakra* translates to wheel or disk. In yoga, meditation, and Ayurveda, this term refers to wheels of energy throughout the body. There are seven main chakras, which align the spine, starting from the base of the spine through to the crown of the head. To visualize a chakra in the body, imagine a swirling wheel of energy where matter and consciousness meet. This energy is the vital life force which keeps us vibrant, healthy, and alive.

Every person is conscious to the degree that corresponds with the natural resistance of their nerves and body. Those are the good pacers that keep everyone growing at their own individual speed. Accept them, because your growth may be happening in one of your other bodies, and you may not be consciously aware of it. Balancing the growth in all of the bodies is necessary to keep us alive.

Everyone and everything is in unison with Life's rhythms, and you are exactly where you are supposed to be. Don't try to be where somebody else is.

Becoming more aware and awake, means looking at your programming and purposely changing the parts of it that keeps you from being more conscious. To be more conscious means to be more aware of what you want and to know if what you are doing is still working for you. More awareness gives us more choices about how we live our lives.

If we picture ourselves as a complete circle, ideally, we would be in complete spiritual consciousness, and aware of everything. We would have three hundred sixty degrees of consciousness. Deliberately developing our conscious awareness allows us to see more of life, ours and everybody else's. All development, all progress, has to include both the positive and negative aspects of that area of life. That's the law. You can't have one without the other. That's where the pacing comes in.

The more choices we have, the more life we have available, and the less we live on psychological automatic. Our conscious mind can be taught to take us out of where we are into where we desire to be – which is its purpose.

Next we move on to the third and densest part of the mental body. Its rate of vibration is slower than the sub conscious mind above it, and faster than the unconscious mind residing below it.

1. The super conscious- future time
2. The conscious- now time
3. **The sub-conscious- this life time**
4. The unconscious- the past –the largest

3. The Subconscious Mind – this lifetime and our primary emotional relationships:

The subconscious part of the mind is the home of psychological automatic, and it is the third densest of the four mental body divisions.

The sub conscious part of the mental body is the storage center for all the experiences and expressions of those experiences that have happened to you during this lifetime.

This is where one starts when we choose to change our programming and stop living on "psychological automatic" mode; it's akin to "autopilot", in which little if any thought is present. This is where you explore your early family programming and change the parts that no longer serve your best interests.

The sub conscious mind utilizes mother and father's patterning of your emotional body to keep you living on psychological automatic. When you live on psychological automatic, you take who you are and hang it on a hat rack; you live life through the choices your mother and father made for you. The psychological automatic state of living vibrates at the rate of the dream state, the same rate as Earth. Essentially you are asleep.

The more choices you have, the less you are stuck in your subconscious programming. That's how to recognize when you are making life decisions on your own. If you run out of choices, check to see if you are mired somewhere in your subconscious patterning.

In the spiritual energy arena, the area of subconscious programming lies at the top of the third chakra, and corresponds to the subconscious part of the mental body. The third chakra works with yellow. Mastery of the third chakra means learning to recognize when you are processing other people's thoughts, and how to change that.

Mostly, people change because it takes a huge amount of energy to stay stuck and it gets more and more painful to hold on. To not change is very hard work because all of life is changing constantly. The universe encourages us to make both joyous and sad changes as it spins along. Change is the natural state of our world. People change when they can no longer tolerate the great burden of misery and monotony of staying the same. It takes a massive amount of energy to hold the stuck position and sometimes that energy is just not available. It is usually at this point when people often say, "I have to give up."

This part of the mental body has a huge amount of control and power over our life, and will continue to make all kinds of decisions for us that we may or may not like, until we change it. That is what it is trained to do. And, it will fight us changing it. That's why we procure professional help, the help of a trained therapist or someone.

The sub conscious lies just above the unconscious part of the self. The sub conscious part of the mental body stores the essences of the experiences from this lifetime. The experiences that happened to us repeatedly, or with a lot of intensity or any traumatizing experiences are heavier than the other experiences in this lifetime. They fall down into the unconscious at the end of each lifetime, and the essence, not the details, are stored there and carried over into the next lifetime. This storage vault resides within you permanently and gives you directives when you decide on how your next lifetime is to be lived.

It is important to know how subconscious programming takes place. This is the progression:

The emotional body, the astral body, is kept alive through the emotional energy our mothers fed us. We shared the same environment and a part of how she felt about it was sent to us to process every day of our life in the womb. Every child is born with an emotion-carrying umbilical cord attached to their mother on the astral planes, so that she can feed them emotional energy. The emotional body energy cord is much like the umbilical cord attached to their mother in the physical womb. We would not have survived without this connection and this cord. We would have died.

The astral umbilical cord connection stays in place from birth to puberty. The child's emotional body survives by processing a part of the mother's emotional energies until they reach puberty. Then the child begins to develop their own emotional body. Gradually, and many times not too gracefully, the child's emotional attachment to mother loosens and drops away, just as the physical umbilical cord shrivels up and drops away after the physical birthing. This process impacts mother and child most of all. Mother has to take her own emotional independency back because the child begins to develop their own emotional independency through individuation while mother loses someone to process much of her emotional energy for her. Sources of joy, pain, and anger for all.

Breaking free of the emotional state of our parents, and their relationship with each other, particularly mother, is the emotional task that carries the child through puberty. Being attached to mother and processing her emotions may have meant we had to process a lot of fear or other negative emotions every day of our lives for the first thirteen or fourteen years.

Mothers and father's exchanges always create emotions, and children always process them. Some people's fathers were their primary emotional caretakers. If they were lucky, nature and the females around him kept the energy avenues open for him to send the child the needed emotional nourishment.
At puberty, as the child's hormones and endocrine system kicks in, and their own emotional body begins to learn how to process its own energy, they begin to do their own

emotional functioning independent of mother and father. Everything they have experienced and expressed as a child gradually settles into a permanent, automatic wave pattern in the right hemisphere of the brain. That's how subconscious programming is created. That means our mother and father patterns are set up in the genetic coding of our chromosomes, and in the RNA and DNA, which set up the patterning for the proton and electron in every atom of our being.

Every day, for the rest of our life, in reaction to all situations, this permanent, hard-wired energy system sends emotional energy into our emotional systems; the endocrine, adrenals, and there are many more. We process that energy automatically until we set about changing it.

At that point, we begin to work on our personal psychological stuff, so we can come to know the essence of ourselves. That is what we came here to do; that is what we yearn to spiritually achieve. We yearn to learn how to fully live out our true intentions and to fulfill ourselves in the most complete way possible. In most cases, it takes a trained professional to help us develop and change our systems of thought.

It is an elegant, enlightening, hard, scary, deeply worthy process to wake up and get to know yourself.

Emotions are regulated through the endocrine system, which in turn, releases the hormones in our bodies. Our western culture does not incorporate emotional processes in our teachings. In fact, they are against them.

Our Western cultural systems are not designed to incorporate emotional processes. Those systems oppose them. A large part of the fear of each of the emotions we carry as human beings is primal, and is founded within and upon the ancient taboos against recognizing or expressing emotions. Once, the belief was that emotions would weaken us, and we might not survive as a species. But our emotions are the key to our spirituality and we strengthen that spirituality through our emotional growth work. Our emotional growth connects us to all others and provides the access to the overall, awe inspiring strengths latent in the best part of ourselves.

The decision to change our subconscious programming does not mean we toss it all away. We can't toss it away, because we need it; every family pattern has its own lineage of thoughts and needed survival skills. Everyone in the family has similar thought processes, and we are trained to think along those lines to stay connected to each other.
Also, we are talking about our mental body, the home base of thought processes about ancient truths. It may have taken generations, eons of time to accrue those influences for the many good things in your life you may not recognize yet.

Sexual Abuse:

A child whose mother was sexually abused while the child was in the womb, abused either physically or energetically/emotionally, has to cope with those issues as though they were their own.

Many times an unborn child is forced to learn to bond with and help the perpetrator with their negative, magnetic energies, so they can survive in the womb. This negative course of action, forced on the unborn child, causes a fracture, or an interruption of the natural energy patterns between the mother and child, and stops the child's needs for nurturing from being satisfied.

If a child has been sexually abused before puberty, the emotional cord to the mother on the astral plane may be ruptured, and possibly completely lost. The result is that the natural subconscious programming and its movement into its proper place when puberty starts is altered emotionally. It is very possible that the child may relinquish their emotional attachment to the perpetrator, who then seizes the child's emotional cord of attachment, causing the child to process the perpetrator's emotional energy as well as whatever is left of the mothers.

When a child's body has been stimulated to handle developing sexual energy too early, the child is prevented from the needed, vital dependency on the mother's emotional attachment.

Most perpetrator's patterns are secretive. They take the emotional essence of innocence from the child, and the child is forced to learning isolation, shame and humiliation instead. **A child has to have emotional energy provided from somewhere in order to survive and it will seek it out, good or bad**.

It is through the mother's emotional attachment that the patterning for emotional and spiritual connection is passed on. If a child's only way of obtaining that energy is through aligning with the perpetrator, then the child will be loyal to them in order to survive. This pattern of dependency on the perpetrator can last many lifetimes. Since most perpetrators are male, a tendency to emotionally favor men can manifest and act itself out in many ways. The child might become programmed to believe that any connection in their life has to begin with sexual behaviors.

On another level, it may be helpful to look at the abuse differently.

Atoms never touch each other, though it looks like they do. The Matter of each atom is surrounded by the electron force, the mother energies, which repel the energies that come near the atom. It's an invisible shock absorber. Though we have the sensation of being touched, it is the force of the electrons in ours and their atoms overlapping and repelling each other.

If we look at it in energy terms, it seems that the neutron in atomic structure, the seat of the Child, never gets touched by the perpetrator's energy. Rather, the electrons in the atom create a spinning force field around the nucleus where the inner child sits,(the neutron) and repels the perpetrator's electron force field. The child is always protected in this manner. That doesn't mean the violation didn't occur; there is still a need for healing. Knowing this from a scientific point of view may bring relief.

Vibrations

We've talked about the different vibrational levels in the mental body but haven't explained what those vibrations are. Before we go further, a basic understanding of these vibrations helps understand their significance. The earth vibrates at approximately 7.83Hz. These vibrations were first measured by physicist Winfried Otto Schumann in 1952. Schumann resonances occur because the space between the surface of the Earth and the conductive ionosphere acts as a closed waveguide. The limited dimensions of the Earth cause this waveguide to act as a resonant cavity for electromagnetic waves in the ELF band. The cavity is naturally excited by electric currents in lightning. Schumann resonances are the principal background in the part of the electromagnetic spectrum[1] from 3 Hz through 60 Hz,[2] and appear as distinct peaks at extremely low frequencies (ELF) around 7.83 Hz (fundamental),[3] 14.3, 20.8, 27.3 and 33.8 Hz.[4]

Human Brain Vibrations

All humans display five different types of electrical patterns or "brain waves" across the cortex.

Our brain's ability to transition through various brain wave frequencies plays a large role in how successful we are at managing stress, focusing on tasks, and getting a good night's sleep. If any of our brain waves doesn't produce correctly, it can cause problems.

There is no single brain wave that is "better" or more "optimal" than the others. Each serves a purpose to help us cope with various situations – whether it is to help us process and learn new information or help us calm down after a long stressful day. The five brain waves in order of highest frequency to lowest are: gamma

---

[1] MacGorman, W. D. Rust, W. David Rust. (1998). *The electrical nature of storms.*

[2] Hans Volland. (1995). *Handbook of atmospheric electrodynamics*, Volume 1, page 277.

[3] Rusov, V.D. (2012). "Can Resonant Oscillations of the Earth Ionosphere Influence the Human Brain Biorhythm?" Department of Theoretical and Experimental Nuclear Physics, Odessa National Polytechnic University, Ukraine

[4] Montiel, I.; Bardasano, J.L.; Ramos, J.L. (2005). "Biophysical Device For The Treatment Of Neurodegenerative Diseases". In Méndez-Vilas, A. *Recent Advances in Multidisciplinary Applied Physics. Proceedings of the First International Meeting on Applied Physics (APHYS-2003) October 13-18th 2003, Badajoz, Spain.* pp. 63–69.

ϖ   beta

ϖ   alpha

ϖ   theta

ϖ   delta

Gamma

These are involved in higher processing tasks as well as
cognitive functioning. Gamma waves are important for
learning, memory and information processing. It is thought
that the 40 Hz gamma wave is important for the binding of
our senses with regard to perception and are involved in
learning new material.

- **Frequency range**: 40 Hz to 100 Hz (Highest)
- **Too much**: Anxiety, high arousal, stress
- **Too little**: ADHD, depression, learning disabilities
- **Optimal**: Binding senses, cognition, information
  processing, learning, perception, REM sleep
- **Increase gamma waves**: Meditation

Beta Waves

These are high frequency low amplitude brain waves that
are commonly observed while we are awake. They are
involved in conscious thought, logical thinking, and tend to
have a stimulating affect. Having the right amount of beta
waves allows us to focus and complete school or work-
based tasks easily. Having too much may lead to
experiencing excessive stress and/or anxiety. The higher
beta frequencies are associated with high levels of arousal.

When you drink caffeine or have another stimulant, your beta activity will naturally increase. Think of these as being very fast brain waves that most people exhibit throughout the day in order to complete conscious tasks such as: critical thinking, writing, reading, and socialization.

- ♣ **Frequency range**: 12 Hz to 40 Hz (High)
- ♣ **Too much**: Adrenaline, anxiety, high arousal, inability to relax, stress
- ♣ **Too little**: ADHD, daydreaming, depression, poor cognition
- ♣ **Optimal**: Conscious focus, memory, problem solving
- ♣ **Increase beta waves**: Coffee, energy drinks, various stimulants

Alpha Waves

This frequency range bridges the gap between conscious thinking and subconscious mind. In other words, alpha is the frequency range between beta and theta. It helps us calm down when necessary and promotes feelings of deep relaxation

- ♣ **Frequency range**: 8 Hz to 12 Hz (Moderate)
- ♣ **Too much**: Daydreaming, inability to focus, too relaxed
- ♣ **Too little**: Anxiety, high stress, insomnia, OCD
- ♣ **Optimal**: Relaxation
- ♣ **Increase alpha waves**: Alcohol, marijuana, relaxants, some antidepressants

Theta Waves

This frequency range is involved in daydreaming and sleep. Theta waves are connected to us experiencing and feeling deep and raw emotions. Too much theta activity may make people prone to bouts of depression and may make them "highly suggestible" because they are in a deeply relaxed, semi-hypnotic state. Theta has its benefits in that they help improve our intuition, creativity, and makes us feel more natural. It is also involved in restorative sleep. As long as theta isn't produced in excess during our waking hours, it is a very helpful brain wave range.

- **Frequency range**: 4 Hz to 8 Hz (Slow)
- **Too much**: ADHD, depression, hyperactivity, impulsivity, inattentiveness
- **Too little**: Anxiety, poor emotional awareness, stress
- **Optimal**: Creativity, emotional connection, intuition, relaxation
- **Increase theta waves**: Depressants

Delta Waves

These are the slowest recorded brain waves in human beings. They are found most often in infants as well as young children. As we age, we tend to produce less delta even during deep sleep. They are associated with the deepest levels of relaxation and restorative, healing sleep. They have also been found to be involved in unconscious bodily functions such as regulating heart beat and digestion. Adequate production of delta waves helps us feel completely rejuvenated after we wake up from a good night's sleep. If there is abnormal delta activity, an individual may experience learning disabilities or have difficulties maintaining conscious awareness (such as in cases of brain injuries).

- ♣ **Frequency range**: 0 Hz to 4 Hz (Slowest)
- ♣ **Too much**: Brain injuries, learning problems, inability to think, severe ADHD
- ♣ **Too little**: Inability to rejuvenate body, inability to revitalize the brain, poor sleep
- ♣ **Optimal**: Immune system, natural healing, restorative / deep sleep
- ♣ **Increase delta waves**: Depressants, sleep[5]

4. The Unconscious – Past Lives

Now we move on to the last part of the mental body–the unconscious. The unconscious part of the mental body resides below the sub conscious. Its rate of vibration is slower than any of the other parts, and it is the largest and densest.

1. The super conscious- future time
2. The conscious- now time
3. The sub-conscious- this life time
4. **The unconscious- –past lives**

When you study genealogy, you are studying the patterns containing both the positive and negative attributes contained in your genetic history. Pay attention, and do not become self- grandiose and overlook the cleverness of your ancestors.

The path to selfhood is a universal, mandatory way of being.

The lessons we learned through the mistakes we made each lifetime are stored in the unconscious part of our mental

---

[5] http://mentalhealthdaily.com/2014/04/15/5-types-of-brain-waves-frequencies-gamma-beta-alpha-theta-delta/

body. All of our past life essences are stored there. That is why it is so heavy and large. This is the home base, the largest part of the mental body. The unconscious is your personal storage center, and, it links your mental body directly into the collective unconscious.

You contact this part of yourself through addressing the issues you are dealing with this lifetime–your subconscious programming. As soon as those issues start getting addressed, you are able to work more effectively with the unconscious part of your Self.

The unconscious part of the mental body is the storage center for the Essences of all the experiences and the expressions of those experiences from every life you've ever lived. Those Essences, (capital E by the time they reach this location) create the results of our personal evolutionary process, both positive and negative.

The most powerful, most intense, or repeated events, both negative and positive, that occurred each lifetime were stored in your sub conscious, then that Essence, (not the details) gained density, and eventually dropped down into your unconscious mind and is then stored there.

It is the number and weight of those stored essences that causes the unconscious part of the mental body to be to be the densest, largest, and slowest in vibration. This part of the mental body's vibrations matches the Earth's, and the collective unconscious living on Earth, which includes us. Our sleep vibration is equivalent to the Earth's vibration, and for this reason we are able to access our unconscious state and dream and heal and participate in countless other activities (throughout the universe, too) while in our sleep states. We are all in this together!

We have made many mistakes in our personal evolutionary process so we could learn from them. The essence of those lessons causes the polarity (the relative orientation of poles; the direction of a magnetic or electric field)[6] of the unconscious to be generally negative. This is natural.

The Files of lifetimes are stored in your unconscious:

Your unconscious "state" activates and comes to life when one of the essences, or "files" stored in it, is opened. There are several stimuli that activate a file.

1. Phobias, defined as exaggerated usually inexplicable and illogical fears of a particular objects, class of objects, or situations,[7] are so powerful that they absolutely over power our sense of logic, so much so that we not likely to repeat the experience.
For example: Phobias, which are powerful unconscious fears, are so strong they are absolutely over powering; the phobic person can't stand to repeat the experience.

If you experienced one event in enough lifetimes, for example, being burned to death or drowned, then when you are near fire or water in this lifetime, the unconscious going releases the **Essence** (not the details) of those past life experiences, and you will be afraid. That activated Essence then travels up through the subconscious mind, stimulating the patterns in the subconscious that deal with survival situations. Then the Essence continues to travel up into the conscious mind and at the same time, unloads the emotional Essence into the astral body and you feel it in

---

[6] https://www.merriam-webster.com/dictionary/polarity
[7] an exaggerated usually inexplicable and illogical fear of a particular object, class of objects, or situation

your solar plexus and become afraid. Doesn't matter how safe you are, you will feel extremely afraid. At that point, the unconscious has done its job and the circle is complete. The past lives are connected to the present lifetime, and then to the present moment. At the point of completion, you are going to be afraid, whether there is cause in the now time frame or not.

Relationships: Another way the unconscious activates

Sometimes we meet someone we have known many lifetimes. Stored in our unconscious is an Essence file on them. This file contains the essence of all the experiences we have had with this person throughout all of our lifetimes so far. The file opens because its Essence has been stimulated by meeting that person again. The Essence releases, and travels up through the unconscious mind, up through the subconscious mind, then on up into the conscious mind. At the same time that is happening, the endocrine system picks up the Essence of the feelings you had about the person, and sends them to be felt in your astral body, and in the solar plexus of your physical body. When the conscious mind starts receiving those energies, you begin to react to that person in current time, from the Essence of the past energies you carry about them. At times, your reactions or theirs that may seem unusual.

When you come in contact with people you have known in many other lifetimes, there is a great desire to continue to be with that person to gain completion. But the other person may or may not recognize your need to do that, and may or may not want to focus on the energy between the two of you this lifetime.

No matter who we are today and what values we carry in this lifetime, we each have access to the unconscious part of the self. We live with it every day, whether we are conscious of it or not. It is reflected in the mass consciousness working in all the bigger things around us, including weather and wars. The unconscious part of the self we each carry gives us our permanent attachment to the deeper, larger experiences and understandings of life.

Being born and dying are the strongest experiences we will ever have, and we repeat those experiences every lifetime. We have that in common.

All the parts of the mental body interact and exchange in vital ways that affect all areas of our life time. Future, past and present are all connected to and are anchored in the unconscious part of the timeless Self we are.
As we come to recognize this, our lives change for the better. We begin to redefine our limits and grow a larger kind of compassionate caring for ourselves and the world around us.

All animals are associated with the various aspects of the unconscious, as are the fortune teller, the story teller, the Shaman, dreams, death, Darth Vader, Gotham, Batman, Sherlock Holmes, sleeping, hypnotic trances, loud noises, mantras, chaos, hymns, and rituals.

Soul Mates: Energy connections to other people:

Here's the soul mate part. Ha ha! We are going to look at the time frame connections that happen with us and other people on the energy planes:

Why do we get intense feelings for another?

Astral, Mental, and Soul Mates:

Most people have heard about the concept of soul mates and what happens that causes us to react at the time of "reconnection". Now let's look at the different types of energy planes where these time frame connections happen. There are three primary types of mates. These are:

- ෆ Astral
- ෆ Mental
- ෆ Soul Mates

Astral Mates

There are astral mates that you get along with in your feeling nature. To have an astral mate, you have to have energy ties with them on the astral plane. Usually what has happened is that you have had a ceremonial or ritualized connection to a person that lasted a long time during a lifetime such as marriage. Many astral mates marry. The encounter, for whatever length of time in whatever way during a lifetime, has to have happened at least three times in different lifetimes. With astral mates, sex is great, but when you try to talk, you have little to say.

Mental Mates

With mental mates you have both an astral tie and a mental tie. It takes at least six lifetimes to gain the kind of development necessary to accomplish this kind of mating, which is a meeting of both the minds and the feeling nature of both parties. There is an energy progression, utilizing lifetimes to build these connections. You can be a successful business partner with this person, or enjoy learning and doing things together like a school buddy.

However, you may or may not be in agreement with each other about spiritual things or expressing sexuality.

Soul Mates - or higher earth mates:

There are lower, middle, and higher Earth mates. Higher Earth mates have married the other person in twelve to fifteen lifetimes. That is what it takes to create the spiritual ties with each other on the higher levels of energy.

It takes at least twelve lifetimes to build that deep connection, with those lifetimes being spent together in a ceremonial or ritualized fashion, such as marriage. Usually, the more time connections, the more depth and density the relationship has, but not always. Sometimes, one soul mate does not recognize the other one in a given lifetime. They may have chosen a different priority to focus on during that lifetime and they may be the same or a different gender.

The thing is, with a soul mate, you don't always come in with the same karmic plans. There can be sex, or a great platonic love between soul mates. Both work for them. Many times, they come together to forward a "Cause". What this really is, is a forwarding of energy into the future. Soul mates are chosen to do this because the idealistic rate of vibration is high enough to mentor the energy into the future "plan".

You may be, simultaneously, astral, mental, and soul mates and that relationship may be positive or negative in your point of connection with them in this life time. The other lifetimes times you spent with them may be positive or negative, depending on the karmic balance needed.

With a soul mate, you are on the same spiritual path. Your intention and purpose in the lifetime are supported by the other person. It doesn't need to be spoken. You usually get along with them physically, mentally, and emotionally.

It is said that everyone is looking for the other half of themselves, so they feel complete. There will always be a certain kind of intensity when you sense your soul mate is near, however, you may or may not connect this life time.

It used to be true that almost everyone's soul mate was on the planet. Now, because the Schumann Resonance has increased, the help being given to the planet by a lot of people with a great deal of spiritual knowledge, and information that have come here to help the changes take place at this time, a lot of soul mates choose not to manifest together. Many soul mates come together and split apart because it's so difficult on the physical plane to live a spiritual life together.

Soul mates are always connected to each other, whether they have manifested onto the planet or are living elsewhere in the universe.

Aristotelian Logic and the Mental Body

Aristotelian Logic is a tradition of philosophy that takes its defining inspiration from the work of Aristotle. This school of thought is in the modern sense of philosophy, covering existence, ethics, mind and related subjects. After a great and early triumph, it consolidated its position of influence to rule over the philosophical world throughout the Middle Ages. Aristotelian logic still remains the foundation for much of the world's current thinking processes.[8]

Two dimensional thinking has been maintained through the sky god religions, who insist that this kind of thinking is spiritual. Organized, patriarchal, religious corporations have slowed the shift to equality between men and women through linking spirituality to women being of lesser value than men.

Equality

When you do harm to a man, woman or child, you are harming that structure inside each atom of your own Being. When the Dual Nature of a person, the male and female residing within us, is not recognized as being of equal importance, when emotional logic is not recognized as being as important as mental logic, we are lessening the power and health of our personal Being and those of our future generations.

---

[8] Louis F. Groarke; Aristotle: Logic; Internet Encyclopedia of Philosophy; http://www.iep.utm.edu/aris-log/

Joseph Campbell linked Aristotelian logic with mechanistic science, two-dimensional thinking, and the first, second, and third chakras in his book, Myths to Live By.

Our society still remains, to an uncomfortably high degree, boundarized by Aristotelian logic. Businesses, sciences, and medical professions insist on using Aristotelian logic when defining reality. This system is the finest flowering of the patriarchal view of the world.

Aristotle, during his lifetime, propounded the rules for the primary thinking style that we still use today. These rules confine our minds to creating within specific boundaries. If we step outside of those boundaries, it is thought that we are stepping into the unknown.

Aristotelian logic limits a person's world to a very simple two dimensional mental plane. While it sounds like it follows the causal energy body, it in effect, strangles it. When followed exclusively, this system ignores the emotional and spiritual needs of groups as well as individuals.

Aristotle was a Greek philosopher who was most interested in a two-dimensional polarized world view, such as good - bad, heaven - hell, and black - white thinking. This type of thinking leaves no room for solutions past two-dimensional thinking. This thinking would work fine if people were computers. The problem is, because the mind is multidimensional, two-dimensional thinking confines it to a modality that does not work in the complex world we live in today.

This polarized thinking evolved slowly, over a period of time beginning around 2500 B.C, at the same time the demise of the matriarchal system, and the rise of the patriarchal system was taking place.

The patriarchal system began the birth of linear thinking in the same time period that the matriarchal, circular thinking modalities began to fall back into the past, forgotten, banned, and ignored. Most of the physical representations of matriarchal thinking were destroyed by the incoming patriarchy. As a result, the primitive, timeless, and powerful rituals that ordered the unconscious part of ourselves were lost to our consciousness as human beings.

We have many examples in our society today of the failure of Aristotelian logic to solve problems in our everyday world.

For example, a classic situation in which Aristotelian logic fails is in the case of divorce. It may make perfect mental logic for one party to stay in the house the couple lived in, in terms of the physical considerations within this system of mental logic. In order to understand why the couple may both choose to move, you have to step outside the boundaries of Aristotelian logic, and look at a system of emotional logic that takes into account the emotional disadvantages of either one of the parties staying in the house.

In the middle ages when church leaders attempted to use Aristotelian logic to define spirituality, instead of addressing the soul's knowledge, they stayed mental, and became overly involved with questions such as, "How many angels can sit on the head of a pin?"

EINSTEIN left this system of thinking in order to develop a different picture of reality.

"No problem can ever be solved from the same level of consciousness that created it."

JOSEPH CAMPBELL said, "Read Myths. They teach you that you can begin to turn inward, and you begin to get the message of the symbols. Read other people's myths, not those of your own religion, because you tend to interpret your own religion in terms of fact. But if you begin to read the other ones, you begin to get the message.".

State of the art research in physics today demands the abandonment of the Aristotelian system of thinking in order to explain reality.

American businesses have traditionally been strictly boundarized by Aristotelian logic. In the past, we were able to deal with other human needs by limiting businesses to men, and assigning the fulfillment of emotional needs to women and children within the home. Given the right-wrong, yes-no, male-female configuration of the patriarchal, Aristotelian system of logic, it was inevitable that the greater value would be placed on the male business world.

In a lesser patronizing value, this thinking achieved its zenith in nineteenth century America. The Industrial Revolution separated mankind emotionally from his means of making a living. Inhumane treatment of workers during the Industrial Revolution contributed to the rise of the women's movement in an attempt to swing the pendulum back the other way.

The system of logic in use forms the language of the culture. Many linguists have long recognized that language defines and limits our reality. One of the weaknesses of this movement and all movements towards an equal humanity, is the fact that our very thinking is limited by the effect these old, logic systems have on our language.

A split in the Aristotelian logic occurred around the fifteenth century, when the printing press came into use. Books began to be mechanically produced and became more and more available to people. Written information began to expand people's world view. Relationships between men and women began to be examined through literature as the "Romantic Era" was ushered in. This era came into full bloom during the sixteenth century and lasted for several hundred years. Before the "romantic era", only one modality of thought about women was in place. Because women had lost the power they had during the Matriarchal Era, they had been reduced in status to slaves or animals, not as human beings. None of them were believed to possess a soul of their own. They had no rights except for those given to them by men, and they were mentally classified as sub human.

During the 1600's, through the influence of the written word, women began to be able to qualify for humanity, that is, if they met specific criteria. This meant that they had a soul. The women who qualified for this position had to maintain an elevated position of sacrifice, behavior, and moral codes that were strictly defined by the men of the era. These codes of behavior insisted that these women not express themselves. They were to be given power based on men's control of their energy. They were to be small, demure, and look and dress and act only as dictated by the clergy and the upper classes of men.

Only a small, select group of women could qualify. The rest of the women, meaning almost all of them, retained their sub human status. Unconsciously and unfortunately, this practice continues today, through media and advertising practices. We still see the approval of only ten percent of the women of the world as being acceptable to men.

For generations, a most popular doll has been handed to little girls to play with. This doll has unrealistic physical measurements, yet it is purchased and given to girls with the spoken or unspoken expectation that they strive to look like it. This doll has no personality and is a molded piece of plastic. This is only one of the many ways that little girls are taught to be unconsciously dissatisfied with who they are.

The defining of most of the therapies in use today are based on the assumption that the world view that shifted for ten percent of the people in the 1600's, shifted for everyone. It does look at the very clear possibilities that this is no longer the case, and in so doing it has carried forward the Aristotelian, linear modality of thinking—almost intact—into present day.

Most of the therapy models in use today were defined by men without the input of women. The larger percentage of the therapies were developed for the control of women, because women, as it would naturally follow, were the ones who suffered most in all ways from the changes that the Patriarchal era brought in, mentally, physically, emotionally, and in their souls.

Men considered themselves compassionate when they locked women into back rooms and later into mental hospitals, rather than look at their historical, basic need for maintaining their male power, which was what truly motivated them. Since most of the healers were now called doctors and were men, there was open agreement about the development of an ongoing, powerful system including jails, hospitals, mad house institutions, schools, and therapies to keep anyone who stepped out of line with the approved modality of linear thinking, dis-empowered.

Today's healing systems need to take into consideration the long-term history of the interaction between men and women. This means going back in time to the beginnings of what we know about both men and women, as it relates to time, and developing and healing the history of the treatment men and women have received at each other's hands since that time.

These practices have become almost genetic because they have been passed down through so many generations and have become such a powerful part of the collective unconscious. The deepest wells of self-hate and self-love cannot be healed until people understand that their internal nature contains both masculine and feminine natures; it always has, it always will, and that there is a history of that interaction and the results of that interaction residing within each human being.

When we begin to examine the history of men and women as we know it on this planet, we are examining how we have treated our own internal nature throughout the recorded time humans have been here. Our world history is also our personal history / herstory. Without taking this larger world view into consideration, we are at a loss to understand the more expansive and truly inclusive nature of healing.

Those persons in our society who strive for a different understanding of reality, must do everything possible to expand their reality past the strictures of Aristotelian logic.

One of the advantages of embracing a multi-dimensional view of reality, is that it is possible to eliminate the kind of right-wrong thinking that gives rise to most human disagreements, fights, and wars. The ultimate humanness envisioned in the myth of Genesis is when Adam and Eve made the decision to expand their conscious awareness of life by taking a bite of the "apple". This may have been a positive ritual that gave them the chance to move past two-dimensional thinking. The misconstrued idea that Eve was evil and tempted Adam, comes straight out of patriarchal thinking.

It is based in the fear of going past two-dimensional thinking, and allowing the rejected circular thinking to take its proper and much needed place in our world. The true message in the Adam and Eve story indicates that the zenith of self-awareness would be embracing our humanness in its entirety, by combining both male and female systems, therefore, combining both patriarchal and matriarchal systems.

One of an individual's first steps in this process is to recognize the limitations as well as the advantages of Aristotelian logic. Throwing out the patriarchal view of life and how it works is de-evolvement. Throwing out the straight line does not work. Throwing out the matriarchal world view, the circle, does not work either. The work is to combine the two. Without a good form of exchange between the two genders, internally and externally, we cannot move into further dimensions of Life and Spirituality.

Mental Body Drivers

The mental body develops three root faculties:
- ϖ Emotion
- ϖ Intellect
- ϖ Will

It takes the use of Will to develop the energies that vibrate slower than the soul body. In each of the four bodies there are seven chakras. Each of these chakras match a Kingdom of Matter for developing the character traits in accordance to that chakra. Some of the values being developed are:
- ϖ Beauty
- ϖ Truth
- ϖ Goodness

Planets within each universe which have all four planes, physical, astral, mental, soul, all have life on them and follow this order:
- ϖ The Cosmos,
- ϖ Universe
- ϖ Galaxies
- ϖ Solar systems
- ϖ Planets

Each are all divided by quadrant and sector systems. It is said that Earth resides in sector six, 4th quadrant.

The activities of each part of the mental body are affected by the participation of the rest of the time frames. When issues are divided up into time frames, it is easier to divide them into their areas in terms of where and when they happened. Then we can look for the healing modalities and the appropriate helpers and healers who work in that area.

Problems can be addressed and healed from any level. That's one of the big secrets we are not supposed to know. For example, use a regression ritual for past life issues when the problem resides in the unconscious, or a past life. That's soul level and above stuff, so you would address the unconscious part of yourself.

You could start praying and have others pray for you. Create and participate in rituals. Find Shamans and past life regressors. See a Seer and have your future told. Let the dead die off so it can turn into fertilizer to help create you again in a new way. Get the worst predicted, the more dire the prediction, the better the fertilizer for creating a new future for you or someone else.
Don't dictate to the Universe. It is the boss. Accept its findings. Let your life come full circle by going forward into the future by purposely ending the old future myths and creating new possibilities.

Gaining Personal Divinity

It is very important to learn how to think when your soul calls you out to learn how to do it. When it is the correct time for learning how to think, your soul will connect you into your future through your objective observer. In energy terms this is called the higher causal body. This body lies between the higher mental planes and the lower soul planes. This is the beginning of the God-Self. The more you develop it, the less you live on "psychological automatic". This is the part of the self that attaches us to our personal Divine self–to our personal divinity.

The mental body, on Earth in this age, receives more support for growth than all of the other bodies combined.

"What to think" and "How to think" are very different procedures. The mind of the Mental Body is here to learn how to think. If you know how to think, much more is possible for you.

Though we assume that we live in a "What to think" world, we really live in a "How to think" world. How to think has always been available to us, and is at this very moment. As we wake up and learn how to think, our energy patterns become more and more harmonious with Nature and the universal laws.

As we grow from babies into children, we are taught "What to think". Everything is attached to a label. The bigger part of this process begins with learning to name things and people. It has to be that way. As we grow older, we are still taught "What to think" about the different parts of life situations we encounter. Examples of this would be: "If you fall down, you get back up!", "Mind your manners!" etc. Our philosophies about what Life is about, are instilled in us early on, and we are told what is good and bad, who our friends should be, and how to behave in any situation. It is a survival necessity to learn these things in this way at that stage or our lives.

"What to think" is a ritual of learning by rote. It is done this way for survival as well as other reasons. We take in the information, attitudes and beliefs without questioning them, and recite them at the appropriate times.

"What to think" resides in the sub conscious programmed part of us. It is its home, and we need the structure it provides to stay safe and live in our world when we are children. Moreover, it gives us a solid base to rely on when it comes time to nudge our conscious awareness from its sleep.

When we reach puberty, and begin the struggle to gain our own emotional independence from our parents programming, "What to think" becomes hardwired into our brain. We keep this hard-core patterning, though it is affected by time, environment, the world, and our other personal changes. But a time comes when we know that if we want to mature, we have to begin think for ourselves. As we deliberately wake ourselves up to more choices than before, we begin to create our own lives the way we want them.

We are not what we were told we were in the "what to think" system. We never were. By group agreement, we learned a whole lot of things that aren't true–things that do not work for us.

The "what to think" system stifles the individual growth of perceptions and personal truth. The use of imaginative, creative solutions, the possibilities each person carries, is not allowed because it causes growth and change in family relationships.

Yet the sub conscious programming is just doing its job; not being good or bad, just keeping you on psychological automatic, which is what it is programmed to do. And it doesn't want to change and will fight you not to.

The mind runs the show for most people.

Most people's subconscious part of their mental body contains a lot of negativity, but their conscious minds do not, which is used to live in "now" time. As you begin the process of learning "how to think", you realize how very different those two parts of the mental body are from each other. As "What to think" loses its hold and has to share power, as is appropriate, it becomes "psychological automatic" fertilizer, and the foundational frame of reference it was always meant to be.

The Future: The Objective Observer; The Gaining of Our Divine Purpose

The ability to distance the self from too much closeness is called objectivity.

Concepts are formed through the process of expansion of an idea. A concept is a group of ideas that began with a single idea that expanded. For example, this is a town, in a state, surrounded by states, in a country.

The objective observer is the mental body part of us that is attached to the beginning of our personal divinity. Our physical, astral, and mental bodies are attached to and tie into the objective observer. They receive constant neutral data reports from the objective observer. As we learn to work with our objective observer, our energy shifts into higher planes.

The objective observer is not our analytical mind, which constantly feeds us data through learned thought processes. It never tells us what decisions to make, that's left up to your sub conscious programming.

The objective observer—the causal body—is attached to our awakened areas on the soul planes. This part of our self has the most control over our personality. This is the part of the self that uses the personality as a tool for experiencing and expressing the gaining of our divine purpose. This is the part of us that we, with help, teach to see, in three hundred sixty degrees, in the unseen realms our being resides in. The objective observer's residence is where your consciousness and your life force reside and expand from.

Protecting and Healing Your Mental Body - Creating a Christmas tree

Visualize this: Make a grid of the mental body, not the brain. Located every inch and a half apart, is a golden light which is a sphere of enlightenment, a faculty or an attribute that has been developed by you. Change this grid until it resembles a beautiful Christmas tree filled with gold lights. Each golden light is a faculty or an attribute that represents at least one of the available fifty-five mental attributes to be gained. They may be a capacity, an attribute, a virtue, or another one of the many abilities that are available on the mental planes. As you gained more awareness, more of the golden lights turned on, and the more awesome and beautiful your mental body became.

Admire your beautiful mental body.

After awhile, look closer at the grid. There are missing lights. Where did they go? Did you give them away? Or are there ones you don't use? The less the lights are on, the less you are awake. Hue-mans give these golden lights away to others all the time without knowing it. A stranger might walk by and take one without either of you knowing it.

Remedy?

Close your eyes. Take a deep breath. Imagine yourself in an old auditorium with wine red drapes hanging along both sides of the room from ceiling to floor. You are standing up front on the stage. It is made of wood flooring. You look out into the auditorium, and see many empty seats attached to each other in rows. They have rounded wood backs, and are lined inside with maroon velvet. You are standing behind an old-fashioned wood podium that has scrolls on the sides. To the right of you is a table stacked with rolled up papers tied with a ribbon, like graduation certificates. Somehow you know that each rolled up paper bears the description of a mental attribute, or other mental energy, that you need to return to someone. How many rolled up papers are there depends on how many it is time to return to their owners, who may or may not even know that their mental faculties were gone until now. You also know that before that can happen, you need to take back your own mental attributes and other mental energy stuff from other people.

Take a deep, slow breath and let it out as two angels step up and stand on each side of you. They are large, about eight or nine feet tall, and are from the Shields Brotherhood. Place both your hands on the podium and mentally call the people who are to return your mental attributes to you at this time. Ask them to gather in the auditorium.

The double doors to both sides of the auditorium open and people start filing coming in. Some you know, many you don't. Some are angry or embarrassed… or are having other emotions. Don't get hooked…the angels are there to take care of that…. The double doors close automatically after the last person comes in.

Ask all of them to sit up front. Wait until they are all seated. Then see the angels step forward as the first person stands up, walks up the left side steps onto the stage, and passes in front of you, giving you back your mental faculty or other mental energy. There is no conversation. No explanations are necessary. They go down the steps on the right side of the stage and leave the auditorium.

When all of them have passed by you and are gone, then it is time for you to call in the people that you need to give the papers on the table to. Ask them to come into the auditorium and sit up front. One at a time, each one comes up on stage to receive their mental faculty back from you. Some of them may be angry at you or don't want to come up on the stage. You may be surprised at who is there.

When it is done, and they have all left, thank the angels for protecting everyone and for seeing that the procedure was done properly.

State three times. "Let all of this be done in the highest karmic good of all concerned."

Close your eyes and let the angels escort you off the stage and out of the auditorium. The doors close behind you. Thank whoever comes to mind, then leave and go home. You will feel the good difference. Do this as needed.

Chakras

The higher mental planes reside just below the lower soul planes of energy. They have a relationship with each other and work together.

Most of the Eastern philosophies and religions believe that to the degree that our chakras are open, is the extent to which we know our God. Their disciplines are based on mantras and meditations, which give receptivity to opening these energy transformer centers.

In the Eastern philosophy, it is believed that it is in the giving up of the doing that one comes to know their God self. In the Western philosophy, it is believed that it is in the doing that one comes to know God. Both philosophies focus on opening the chakras.

Thinking is a process. It shuts off the more we become active. When we are busy physically or emotionally, the part of us that meditates on life doesn't do anything. But it becomes very active when we are still. It kicks in and goes to work!

The unconscious part of the self is attached to the greater collective unconscious and to our inner person. The busy conscious awareness part of the self does not like to give over control to it. The unconscious is loaded with negatives. That's what gives it its weight and size and makes accessible all the ages that have ever been. The unconscious is attached to our inner person.

To meditate successfully, one can use a positive short and simple mantra such as "I release, let go, and let God," or "Peace is with me."

Our genetics can be changed through meditation. That requires entering the area of the mental body and knocking on the door through meditation. That's how powerful it can be. One can change a pattern or issue that seems impossible to overcome, searching out our spiritual genetic patterning and develop stronger pattern recognition through meditation.
Use guidance to learn how to get there, then do it yourself. It's your gateway to more than can be imagined.

The song "My Sweet Lord" by George Harrison is about this process.

My sweet Lord
Mm, my Lord
Mm, my Lord
I really want to see you
Really want to be with you
Really want to see you, Lord
But it takes so long, my Lord
My sweet Lord
Mm, my Lord
Mm, my Lord
I really want to know you
I really want to go with you
Really want to show you, Lord
That it won't take long, my Lord
(Hallelujah)
My sweet Lord
(Hallelujah)
My Lord
(Hallelujah)
My sweet Lord
(Hallelujah)
I really wanna see you
I really wanna see you
I really wanna see you Lord
I really wanna see you Lord
But it takes so long, my Lord
(Hallelujah)
My sweet Lord
(Hallelujah)
Mm, my Lord
(Hallelujah)
My my my Lord
(Hallelujah)
I really wanna know you
(Hallelujah)
I really wanna go with you

(Hallelujah)
I really wanna show you, Lord
That it won't take long, my Lord
(Hallelujah)
Mmm
(Hallelujah)
My…

Source: LyricFind

Songwriter: George Harrison

My Sweet Lord ©The Bicycle Music Company

www.ingramcontent.com/pod-product-compliance
Lightning Source LLC
Chambersburg PA
CBHW071136100726
47908CB00008B/2622